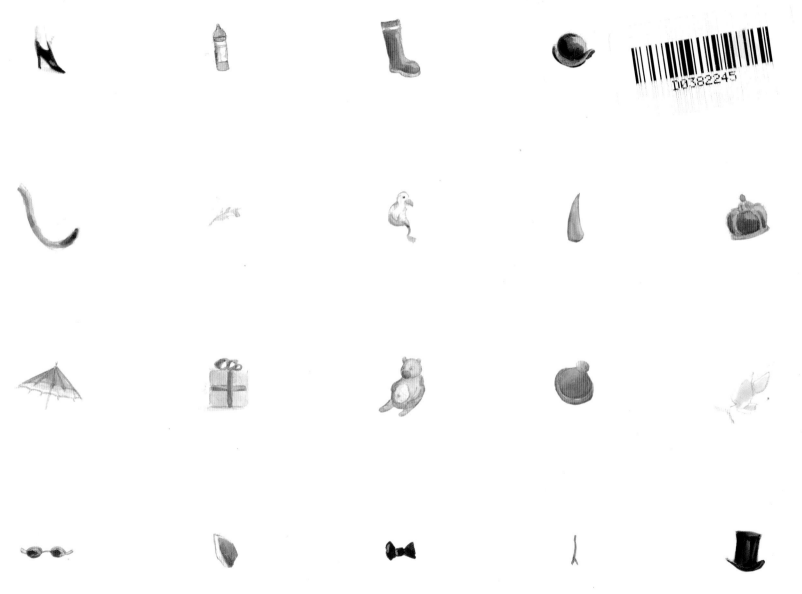

To my wolf, my otter and my three bears

Kane/Miller Book Publishers, Inc.
First American Edition 2009
by Kane/Miller Book Publishers, Inc.
La Jolla, California

Originally published in France by Le Baron Perché, Paris, 2007
Copyright © Edigroup, 2007

For information contact:
Kane Miller, A Division of EDC Publishing
P.O. Box 470663
Tulsa, OK 74147-0663
www.kanemiller.com
www.edcpub.com

Library of Congress Control Number: 2008932256
Printed and bound in China by Regent Publishing Services, Ltd.
2 3 4 5 6 7 8 9 10
ISBN: 978-1-933605-96-8

Not all Animals are Blue

A Big Book of Little Differences

Béatrice Boutignon

WITHDRAWN

Kane Miller

A DIVISION OF EDC PUBLISHING

Who is always eating?

Maybe he'd like to fly instead of walk.

Is there a king?

He is very, very cold. Isn't that strange, for a penguin to be cold?

Do you think that snowball is interesting?

Five Penguins on Parade

Why is she wearing pajamas?

She's having a drink first.

She seems very tall. Perhaps it's her long neck.

And she seems very sad.

She's wearing her eggshell as a hat.

Five Brand New Babies

Who hates to get wet?

He's blowing away!

Whose umbrella shines like the sun?

He likes to feel the raindrops on his face,

But he just likes the puddles!

Five Friends Caught in the Rain

She's wearing her fancy clothes,

And he's carrying all the presents.

Isn't he handsome? What a lovely color.

And what a magnificent hat!

How exciting! This will be her first party.

Five Elephants on Their Way

Who has a bushy tail?

His tail is very elegant.

Why is he a different color?

Do they know what he's hiding?

Doesn't his tail look soft? It's like a pompom.

Five Gentlemen Showing Us Their Tails

Does she **catch** a lot of flies?

Watch out! She has a **black belt**!

Those two do everything together.

Shes **sees** everything clearly.

She loves to sunbathe.

Five Frogs Floating By

What is the baby saying?

Her **high heels** make her even taller!

She is a prima ballerina with the Paris Opéra.

Who couldn't decide which necklace to wear?

She's very flexible.

Five Ladies (and One Baby) Chatting on the Plains

Please don't wake him! He might be angry.

He's the only one eating.

Why is he covering his head?

He has very long whiskers!

Who is a different shape?

Five Big Fellows Staring Straight Ahead

When he's sad, his ears droop down.

He has his jacket on.

Shhhhhh. He's still sleeping.

Whoops! That was a big fall.

He has his favorite toy.

Five Little Donkeys Waking From Their Naps

Look, no hands!

Whose tail is wrapped around?

Who is using both hands and both feet?

One hand and one foot?

One hand?

Five Monkeys Hanging Around

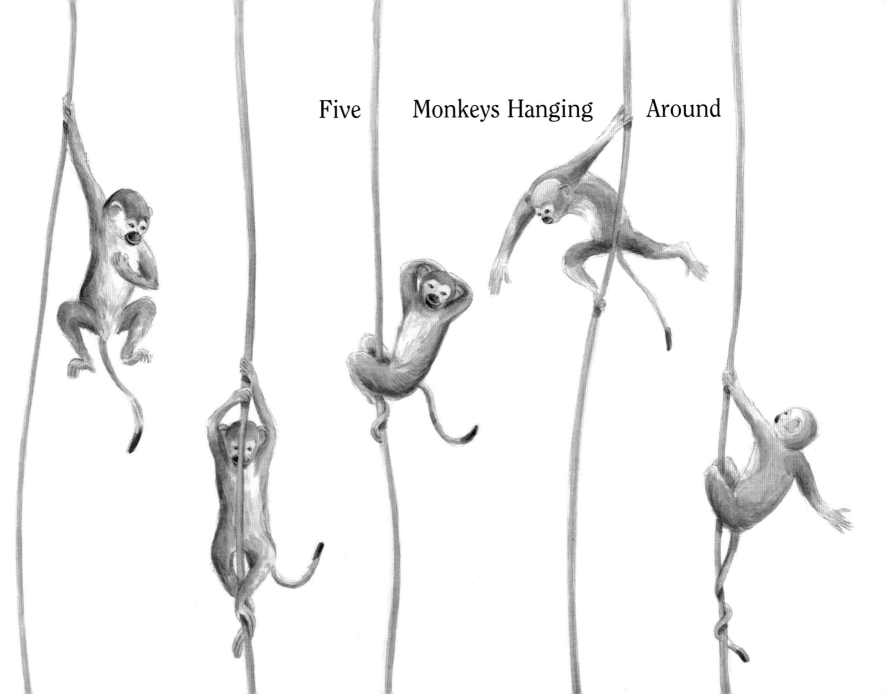

He can't sleep without his blanket.

Who is just pretending to sleep?

Who doesn't have any spots?

She likes to stretch out.

Where is his hat?

Five Puppies Resting in the Afternoon

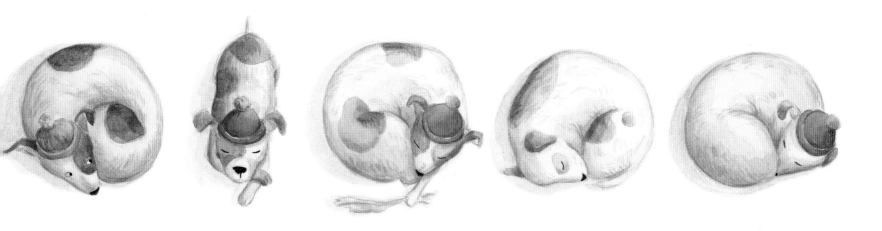

Those two are facing the wrong way.

How pretty! They're wearing matching necklaces.

Whose feathers are not green?

Who look angry with each other?

Who don't?

Five Couples Sitting in the Sun

Who has the best balance?

Who is worried about falling?

That tickles!

He's just relaxing and,

Listening to her tell the story ("The monster was THIS big …").

Five Raccoons Making Mischief

Where is she going?

She's just getting back.

Woops! Hold tight!

Her baby has a special place to sit.

What's going on down there?

Five Storks, Coming and Going

Who is the most serious swimmer?

She's practicing her diving.

A bathing cap!

What a beautiful two-piece bathing suit.

Who likes polka dots?

Five Otters, Ready for the River

He doesn't know which one to open first!

His present is a secret.

She wants to save the ribbon.

Look! Look what she got!

That's a big box.

Five Brothers and Sisters Opening Presents

The Tyrannosaurus is on two legs. He has sharp teeth.

The Triceratops has three horns.

The Stegosaurus has spikes along his back.

The Pterodactyl is the only one who can fly – he's not a dinosaur!

The Diplodocus is the tallest of them all.

Four Dinosaurs and One Pterodactyl

Who is sleeping?

He's trying to say something.

She's tied up in knots!

He has beautiful colors.

He looks like the letter "I."

Five SSSSSSSSSSSSSSSSSSSSSSSnakes

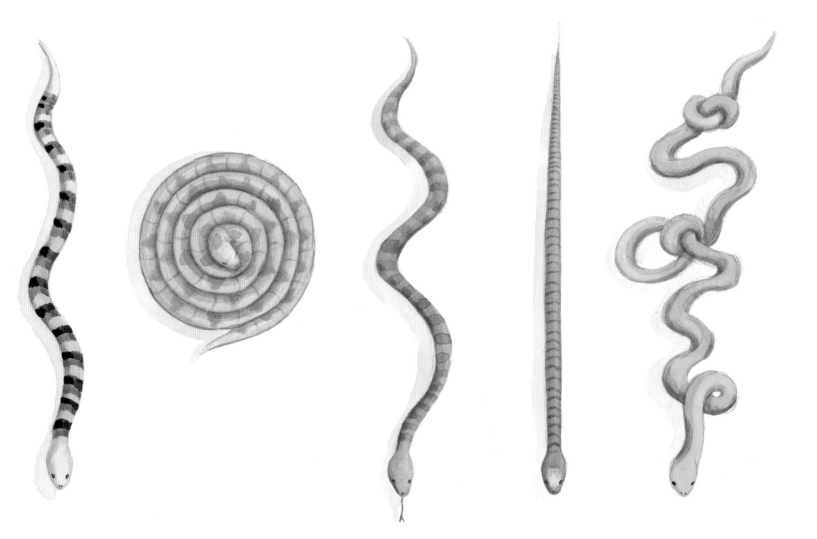

He's a dangerous pirate.

Who is known for his hats?

His colors are world famous.

Doesn't the queen look lovely?

He doesn't like having his picture taken.
He doesn't want to be recognized.

Five Celebrities

He likes to look around.

She's a tour guide – follow the flag!

He can't stop laughing at her.

She is an explorer.

She's wearing her grandfather's bathing suit.
(Maybe that's what the laughing is about.)

Five Dolphins Enjoying the Day

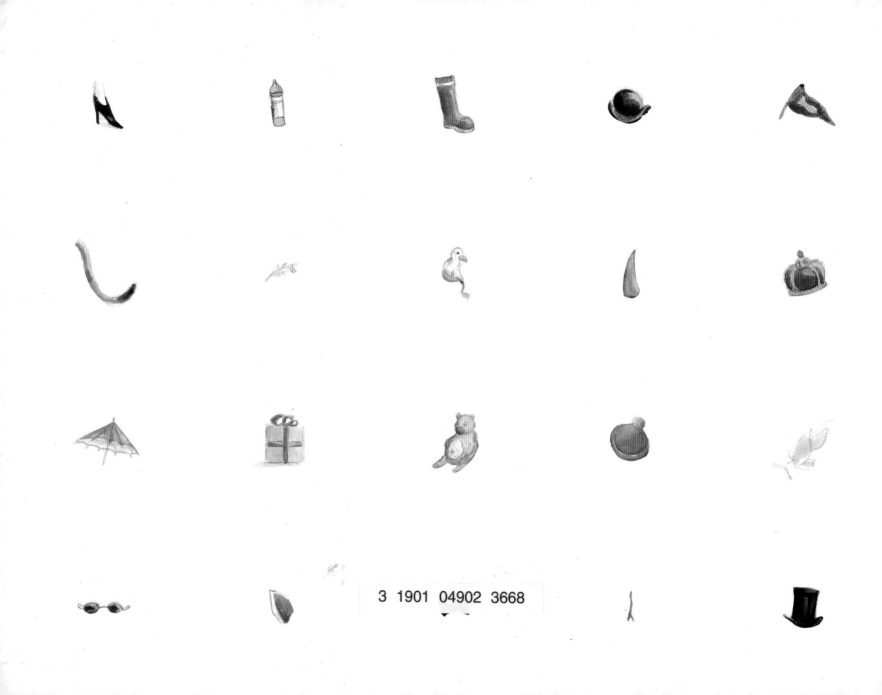